Fake Out

I hear whistles. Fuzz are coming at me
holding clubs. I look around. There is no old
lady with a red hat, a blue coat, a pink dress,
and black shoes — plus a red beard.

Oh, you jerk, I tell myself. You've been
had.

They are all around me now. They have
blue coats, but with buttons, red pants, and
black billy clubs.

I bounce my ball and they stop. I cut fast
and dribble away. I bounce it over the
counter and jump over after it. A crowd forms
to see what's going on. They block off the
fuzz. There is a door at the far end. Exit, the
sign says.

I go out the door with my ball. Then I'm
running and dribbling fast on the sidewalk
and soon I can't hear any whistles behind me.

**Other Apple Paperbacks
you will enjoy:**

Adorable Sunday
  by Marlene Fanta Shyer

The Trouble with Soap
  by Margery Cuyler

Starstruck
  by Marisa Gioffre

A Season of Secrets
  by Alison Cragin Herzig and
  Jane Lawrence Mali

The Alfred Summer
  by Jan Slepian

FRANK AND STEIN AND ME

Kin Platt

AN
APPLE®
PAPERBACK

SCHOLASTIC INC.
New York Toronto London Auckland Sydney

ISBN 0-590-33844-7

Copyright © 1982 by Kin Platt. All rights reserved. This edition published by Scholastic Inc., 730 Broadway, New York, NY 10003, by arrangement with Franklin Watts, Inc.

12 11 10 9 8 7 6 5 4 3 2 1   5 6 7 8 9/8 0/9

1

I'm Jack Hook, as in hook shot. You guessed it. I'm always on a basketball high. It's my game, my life, and I live with the ball.

My old man was a pretty good shooter, real sharp from the foul line. He got me into the game early. He took me to the Forum when I was little to see Wilt and Earl the Pearl. Then later it was Jerry-Mr. Clutch, then Kareem, the wild Harlem Globetrotters and Meadowlark Lemon. Then it was Ice Bird, and now Magic Johnson.

I dribble my ball as soon as I'm off from school — that's Webster Junior High in West Los Angeles. And I dribble it off to bed. I sleep with it, and roll it and spin it. I know some day it will be me at the Forum playing with the Lakers, going down the boards. And if it won't be the home-team Lakers, it will be the Suns or Pistons, Knicks or Hawks.

As I say, it's my game. The proof is, if it wasn't I'd be too dead to tell about it.

What happened is far out. I have this kid sister, Susie. She's smart as a whip. She reads and reads and doesn't know when to stop. She read about this contest for Glop Oil. It's something new for cooking. They want us all to buy some. So you have to write, in twenty-five words or less, why you like Glop Oil. The first prize is a trip to Paris. Is that crazy? A free trip to Paris because of why you dig Glop Oil.

Susie is far out. She writes them, "I like Glop Oil because my plants like it."

And she wins.

But since she never takes a chance of being a dummy, what does she do? She signs my name to it.

When she gets the call that she wins, she doesn't believe it. Then she sees the follow-up letter. It's all real. *"Jack Hook, we are pleased to tell you, you have won first prize — one free trip to Paris."*

Now Susie goes bananas. Paris is what *she* wants — all that French stuff they have there. She yells, "The Eiffel Tower, the art museums, the Left Bank, the weird artists, and the French fries."

So I say, "You take the trip. I couldn't care less. I'll tell them it was you who won." While she is thinking about that, she gets the mumps. The date for the plane is in one week and she is still looking like a football on each cheek.

"Okay," she says. "I blew it with the

2

mumps. You go, Jack. Have it all, and then you can tell me about it."

I'm on my way. I have all my stuff to wear for the week in Paris and my ball. I wouldn't go anywhere without it.

My old man drops me at the airport. The plane is there and set to go. I have my free ticket. An old dude stops me. He has this little wrap-up box. "Take it for me, brother," he says. "It's a birthday cake for my dear old mom who lives in Paris. She will be there."

I can't say no to his mom, can I? "Okay," I say. "How will I know her?" "No trouble," he says. "She will be wearing a red hat, a blue coat, a pink dress and black shoes."

"Right on," I say.

"One thing more," the dude says. "She may be wearing a red beard."

"Hey, man, that's wild," I say. "Your old lady wears a beard? How come?"

"Well," he says, "she started to shave too early."

I have no more time to talk and jive with him about his mom and the fuzz. The lady from Glop Oil is there to see me on the plane. She's a real nice chick, but too old for me now. Maybe she'll still be around later.

The man with the wings on his hat takes us up. The air chicks bring on the food. I eat and eat as if there is no tomorrow. The Glop Oil lady likes how I put it all away. "You never say no, do you," she says.

"No, ma'am," I say.

I sit with my ball and the dude's box for his mom and doze off. When I wake up, the pilot is telling us we are making good time. We will be over Orly real soon.

I turn to the Glop Oil chick. "What is this with Orly? I thought we were going to Paris?"

"Orly is where we land," she says. "It's the name of the airport."

It is dark when we put down. A million lights are all around. The man puts it down easily. The Glop Oil lady taps me on the arm. "Come along," she says. "Here is your free trip to Paris."

We get out and walk and then we line up. "What is this?" I ask.

"Customs," the Glop chick says. "They look over your bag. They don't want anyone bringing in dope."

"I don't dig that stuff," I say.

There is a man at the end of the line. He opens the bags and raps with the people. The Glop Oil lady tells him that I am with her. I am the contest winner.

"Very good," he says. "It is good I speak English for you. What is that package?"

"Oh," I say. "It is a birthday cake for some old dude's old lady. She is coming to meet me here to get it."

"Very good," he says. "So we open it and see what kind of cake she has."

He tears the paper away. He looks down and then up. He blows a whistle. *Beep beep.*

"You are under arrest," he says. "This is no birthday cake. This is grass."

"No way," I say. "The man said it was a cake."

He shows it to me. The man lied.

"Ten pounds of pot," he says. "Marijuana. You are a smuggler, no?"

"Not me," I say. "I was doing this cat a favor."

He blows more on his whistle. Fuzz people start coming over. The Glop Oil chick looks at me. "How could you do this to us," she says. I try to tell her that the dude asked me.

The man now takes my arm. "Now we look at the ball," he says.

I hold it up. "It's only my basketball," I say.

He smiles. He shakes his head. "Very good," he says. "But now that you are a dope smuggler, we must cut up your ball to see if you are also bringing in coke."

"No way," I say. "You don't cut my ball, man."

He tries to take it. "Open it up," he says.

I hold it tight. "No way," I say. "Nobody cuts this ball."

He blows hard on his tin whistle. "*Gendarme!*" he yells.

I look at the Glop lady. She hates me all of a sudden. "Better do what he says, boy. Maybe he will find out it is just a basketball."

"Look," I tell her. "All that is inside this is

air. And if I let him cut it, I am out my best ball."

"Give it to him," she says, "or your free trip is off!"

I hear whistles. Fuzz are coming at me holding clubs. I look around. There is no old lady with a red hat, a blue coat, a pink dress, and black shoes — plus a red beard.

Oh, you jerk, I tell myself. You've been had.

They are all around me now. They have blue coats, but with buttons, red pants, and black billy clubs.

I bounce my ball and they stop. I cut fast and dribble away. I bounce it over the counter and jump over after it. A crowd forms to see what's going on. They block off the fuzz. There is a door at the far end. Exit, the sign says.

I go out the door with my ball. Then I'm running and dribbling fast on the sidewalk and soon I can't hear any whistles behind me.

2

I kept going away from the trouble. It was night and the street people were looking at me with the ball. So, I cooled it, and held it under my arm.

I didn't know where I was to start with, so I couldn't be any more lost. The signs were in French. I didn't know who was following me. I didn't know what they would do if they found me.

I thought of that dumb birthday cake that turned out to be a brick of pot. I should have known that any cat with an old lady who had a red beard wasn't for real.

I had a little money in my pocket from my old man. Maybe I could get somewhere if I knew where to go. What was for sure was I had blown the free trip to Paris for a week. What was even surer was I didn't have enough bread on me to get back home. And my old man wasn't loaded enough to send me the fare. And still worse, even if I did get the money, those funny guys at the airport check-out counters would be waiting for me.

The more I thought about it, the madder I got. It's not right to get in trouble because of doing somebody a favor. And I got the idea that the dude's mom, who was not around when I was checked at customs, might still be hanging around there. I knew now it had to be a man, and the dude just faked me out about his old mom. Okay, so maybe he got held up in a traffic jam and wasn't around in time. Maybe he missed a bus and didn't know what happened to the delivery.

If I found him, and got him to say the delivery was for him, things might still be worked out. The Glop Oil lady might understand how it was, and like me again. The kid sister was home waiting for me to have a good time for her. It would be dumb to lose it all because of one mistake.

I found an alley and cut back to the air terminal. There was another door from the side. I looked through the glass for any fuzz still waiting for me, or the dude with the red beard. But there were so many people around, I couldn't be sure. I didn't want to take the chance of walking in blind and have it happen all over again. All I needed was to be picked up and arrested on my first trip to Paris. That would not be cool.

Then I saw a red hat moving. It was at the far end of the terminal, going out the front glass doors. If it had all the other colors underneath, it was my man. I ran down the alley to the other side of the air terminal.

The bright lights outside the terminal showed me he had it all together. The red hat, blue coat, pink dress or baggy pink pants, ended with the black shoes. And he had the red beard.

A black car was parked at the curb. He stepped into it.

"Hey, man," I yelled. "Hold it!"

If he heard me, he didn't show it. The car door shut. The engine turned over. It took off, coming my way.

I was running to it, yelling. Waving one arm, the other was holding my ball. The car kept coming, picking up speed. It looked as if it was going past me. I stepped off the curb, waving my arm, yelling for him to stop.

The car stopped. But only after it hit me. I remember flying into the air. Then there was a big crunch when I landed. Never do that again, I was telling myself, when the lights went out.

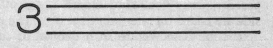

3

When I came to, I was lying down somewhere. I heard a loud rattling noise, and
hoped it wasn't coming from my head. It was
awfully dark. Then I remembered to open
my eyes.

I was on the back seat of a car. My ball
was on my lap. Up front was the dude with
red beard and red hat, and another dude
driving. The car bumped some more. I
groaned.

My man looked back at me. "Ah, he is
coming to," he said.

It was my good luck. The bearded dude
was American, too.

I sat up. "Hey, man," I said. "I want to talk
to you."

He waved his hands. "Don't worry. We are
taking you to a hospital. You can get yourself
hurt running into a car."

"I just found that out," I said.

"When you cross a street, go with the light," he said. "And it is best to do that at the street corner."

"I know all that," I said. "But I had to stop you."

He looked at me. "This is a private car, not a taxi."

"I know that, too," I said. "But I was supposed to meet you. Your friend at the other side sent me."

The driver now turned to look at me. He said something in French to my dude in the red hat. My man said, "What friend? Who are you?"

"I'm Jack Hook," I said, "from Los Angeles. I met your friend there at the airport. He gave me something for you."

He looked interested. "What?"

I shook my head. "First I have to know one thing, man. Are you a man dude with that beard or an old lady?"

He stared at me. "Maybe you hurt your head. A doctor will see you soon."

I rubbed the back of my head. It hurt some but wasn't bleeding. "It's okay. I guess I made a mistake."

He shrugged. "How do I know what friend you are talking about?"

"Because he asked me to bring you a little birthday cake. 'For his old mom,' he said, 'in Paris.'"

He and the other man began talking now,

looking excited and happy. "That must be Ben," he said. "He is a great kidder."

"I found that out, too," I said.

My dude tapped his chest. "At home I am Al but here I am Alphonse. The driver here is Gaston." He looked closely at me. "So where is it, the cake?"

I jerked my thumb back. "At the airport."

He smiled. "You checked it there? Smart boy."

"I'm smarter now," I said. "They opened your birthday cake back there. They found out it was pot instead."

The driver jerked his wheel and just missed a truck. My dude Alphonse shook his head and yelled at him to watch out. "The man at customs opened it?" he asked.

I nodded. "Yeah, man. He called the fuzz down on me. You ruined my free trip to Paris from Glop Oil."

He frowned. "There was oil in with the pot?"

"No, man. The birthday cake was ten pounds of pot. The Glop Oil people were giving me the free trip for winning a contest."

He shrugged. "So you won. You are here, Jack. Have a good time."

"I can't," I said. "They'll be looking for me."

"It's a big city," he said. "You will be like a needle in a haystack, Jack. How can they find you?"

"Well, I was hoping you would set it all straight for me back there," I said.

He lifted his eyebrows. "How will I do that?"

"Well, just tell the man there that the cake was for you. That your friend had this wild sense of humor. Then maybe I'll be off the hook and can go back to the Glop Oil lady for my free week here."

He and the other man began talking fast. It was French, and I didn't dig a word. He pointed out the window. I saw that we were now far out of the city. It looked like the suburbs. There were not many cars, and no houses.

The car swung off into a narrow dark road. We bumped along. The car slowed down and then it stopped. "What's happening?" I asked. "Are we at the hospital?"

"Not yet," my friend Alphonse said. "I think we have a flat tire. Hop outside, Jack, will you, and check the right rear tire."

I got out and walked around the car. It was dark, and only the moon gave off a little light. I put my head down closer to the right rear tire. It looked okay.

The car took off!

"Hey," I yelled. "You forgot me."

A hand waved at me from the front window. The car kept going. I watched the red taillights until they disappeared around a turn.

Then I knew for sure they didn't forget me. They were just leaving me. The flat tire was a gag.

I saved one word for myself. "Dumbbell!" I yelled.

4

I walked back to the main road. It was dark and cold. Those two jokers Alphonse and Gaston didn't come back. It was just me and the moon out there.

A truck came along. I tried to flag it down. The driver didn't see me. He kept on going. I yelled after him. All my yelling did was start dogs barking somewhere.

A car came along going the other way. I didn't care which way I went, as long as I got out of this place. It didn't matter. The car kept on going without stopping. It looked like it wasn't the best time for hitchhiking.

To keep warm, I began dribbling my ball and running down the road. It was really weird, my bouncing a ball, running for a lay-up, and no place to put it.

I came to a fork in the road. I couldn't make out the names on the signs but I dug the numbers. Ten kilometers to one place. Twenty to another. I went with the ten.

I was hungry. I needed food, and a place to sleep. It was ten o'clock at night. I was hoping the ten kilometer road would bring me to a hamburger place. And maybe after that to a nice cheap motel.

If I was with the Glop Oil lady now, everything would be cool. But I wasn't. I tried to remember her name in case I found a phone. She had it on a blue badge with a ribbon she wore on her blouse.

Betty Carter! I saw it now in my mind. But I forgot which hotel we were going to in Paris. I was supposed to know it. I mean, I had seen it written somewhere. But I couldn't remember. Maybe the bump on my head wiped me out.

I kept on walking and dribbling the ball. I was making fancy moves on the lonely moonlit road. I knew that ten kilometers was like a mini-marathon — six plus miles. I could run it in under an hour. But I was too worried to run. I didn't know when I would get out of this all right. What if I came to the end of the ten road and I was still nowhere?

I kept walking and dribbling. I was hoping to hear or see a car or a truck going to someplace. The road curved around. It was narrow, with fields on one side, trees and bushes on the other. I was hoping to find an apple tree, or something, but I didn't see any.

The road turned again. It was uphill, and I

was dragging now. I made myself dribble one more time. I made a fake pass and a reverse lay-up. The ball got away. I went after it. It was going out of bounds, through those bushes. I dived after it.

I got the ball but I was going too fast to stop. Too late I saw that I was at the edge of a mountain. Then I was over the edge. I was rolling down, bouncing, going head-over-heels, trying to grab on and hold onto something.

I remember hitting my head on some rocks, trying to hold onto my ball. It was dark anyway on the mountain. But it got a lot darker all of a sudden. I kept falling and bouncing, but I didn't feel anything anymore.

I knew I was dead.

5

I felt myself moving. Holy cow! I told myself. This has to be the world's record for a fall. But my hands felt worn leather instead of rocks and dirt and bushes. I opened my eyes. I was sitting in a car. How come you're never awake when you get a lift? I asked myself.

A man next to me was driving. He had a black beard, black hat, black tie, black suit, and black shoes. Maybe you died, after all, I said to myself. This has to be the undertaker who came to bury you.

We hit a bump and I groaned. The driver turned. "Ah, so you are all right, young man."

I shook my head slowly, carefully. I was afraid it might fall off. "I'm not so sure about that. I just took a bad fall, man."

He nodded his head, looking ahead to the beam of the headlights on the road. "I know. I found you at the bottom of the mountain."

I was feeling my arms and legs. "I must have broken a million bones," I told him. "I hit everything in sight — and a lot I couldn't see."

He laughed. "I found nothing broken. I looked you over back there. I am a doctor."

I looked at him. He wasn't dressed too fancy.

He read my mind. "I'm a country doctor. Dr. Stein is my name."

I felt better. "Nice to meet you, doc. And thanks for the lift. Are you taking me to the hospital?"

He shook his head. "There is no need. You have some cuts and bruises, but no broken bones. I'll fix you up at my home, my boy." He was speaking English. At least my luck was holding out in some ways.

Suddenly I realized. I was missing something.

"My ball!" I yelped.

He wagged his thumb behind us. "I put the ball in the back of the truck."

I looked around. We were in the cab of a pickup truck. "Are you sure?" I asked. He slowed down. "I can stop, if you want so much to go back to get it."

I remembered the last time I stepped out to check something in the back. I needed this ride. "No, doc. It's okay. I'll take your word for it. I don't go anyplace without my ball."

"Interesting," he said. "You are an American, no?"

I said, "Yeah, I am." He asked me what I was doing in his country. I made it fast. "Alphonse and Gaston," I said. "Do you know those two jokers?"

He shrugged. "I think they are somehow famous, as a team, yes." He took out his watch. "We have not far to go. Another thirty kilometers to my house. Then we talk over what to do with you."

"If we pass a hamburger stand on the way," I said, "I'm buying." I dug into my pocket and came out of it waving a few bills.

He reached behind him, on the shelf of the cab. He pushed a heavy black bag toward me. "If you are hungry, there are some sandwiches inside," he said. "I did not have time to eat."

I opened the bag. There were a lot of doctor's tools. Bottles and little jars. And in a brown bag, some cheese, an apple, half a chicken. I waved the chicken leg. "Don't you want some?"

He shook his head, smiling. "I will eat later," he said, "after I feed Frank."

"Who is Frank?" I said.

"My little boy," he said.

I kept eating. I was making up for the meals I missed. I had gone through everything in the bag, when Dr. Stein pointed ahead. "Ah! We have made good time, young man. There is my house."

I looked up a winding road that seemed to go up forever. I kept looking for a house, but as we got closer, I saw what he meant. It wasn't a house exactly. It looked more like a castle.

"Hey, doc," I said, "business must be good."

He smiled at me. He stopped the pickup truck in front of the "house" and got out. I went to the back of the pickup and found my ball. It was there next to a long wooden box. As I followed him to the door, I heard a horrible wailing noise. It sounded like a wolf.

I froze. "What's that?"

He had his black bag in his hand. He took my arm with the other. "I didn't hear anything," he said.

The long wailing sound came again. It hung in the air. Dark clouds drifted over the moon. The castle looked spooky, like one of those drawings you see in fairy tale books.

"Didn't you hear that?" I asked nervously. "It sounds like a wolf."

He nodded briskly, smiling, hurrying toward the big door. He waved his hand. "Oh, yes. We have some of those out here. It's nothing to worry about."

The door opened. He stood there, waiting for me. I wasn't so sure there was nothing to worry about.

That awful wailing sound didn't come from out there. No way. It seemed to come from *inside* the house.

Dr. Stein's hand touched my shoulder and I jumped. "Come along," he said. "We have to take care of those cuts and bruises." I followed him inside and the door closed behind me.

That free trip to Paris was costing me a lot of sweat.

6

It was as big inside as an armory. It was bigger than my school gym. You could toss a ball twenty feet up and not hit the ceiling. It was my first time inside a castle. It felt cold.

All I wanted was to get some sleep and some food. After that, I had to find a way back to Paris. I would see the Glop Oil lady and get my free trip. I had to get that mess fixed about bringing in the pot. I had to get those inspectors at the customs line off my back.

Dr. Stein took me into a small room. He filled a basin with soapy water and got my hands and face clean. Then he dabbed some stinging stuff over the cuts and bruises. He looked me over under the light.

"You are very lucky," he said. "A fall like that could have killed you. You are the first live one I have found."

I spun my ball. "It's my basketball," I said. "It keeps me in shape."

He looked at the ball. "Basketball?"

"Yeah. It's a game we play back in the states."

He shook his head. "I have no time for games."

"They have teams all over the world now," I said. "Russia and France and Cuba. Don't you ever watch it on TV?"

He looked blank. "Teevee?"

"Man, where have you been?" I said. "Everybody everywhere has got the tube. You know, the TV set."

He shrugged. "Oh, yes, I know of it, but I am too busy to have one. Come along now, and we find something to eat."

We went past a lot of rooms and finally came to the kitchen. There was a big warm stove with pots on it and a long table and chairs. He waved his hand. "Help yourself. I want to see how my little boy is."

"How old is Frankie?" I said.

He rubbed his beard. "About three months old."

"Maybe I can see the kid before I go," I said.

He smiled, walking away. "Perhaps tomorrow." He waved to the stove again. "Eat now. I will get your room ready."

There was stew cooking in one of the big pots, enough to feed a whole team. On the table was bread and cheese. I ate and ate till I got tired of eating. Then I washed the dishes off in the sink and set them on the table to dry.

I went looking for Dr. Stein. There were so many rooms, I didn't know where to find him. The place looked like an old museum that was falling apart.

I opened a big door. Stone steps ran down to a dark cellar, like a basement. I saw a lot of steps but not the bottom. My hand felt the wall for a light switch. There wasn't any, but I saw something glowing. It was a long torch burning. It smelled like tar. That's what people used before lights, in the old days.

I didn't feel brave enough to pick it up and walk down to the bottom. Maybe it's some kind of dungeon, I told myself. Forget it. With your luck, you might trip over a dead body or a skeleton down there.

I didn't feel like calling out for Dr. Stein. I was afraid some other voice might answer. I would have jumped out of my shoes.

I closed the door softly, not wanting to wake anybody up. I'd watched this kind of scene on late TV. In the old movies some jerk always goes down to look in the old cellar. The door closes behind him. It's locked and he can't get back out. He keeps going down further waiting for his heart attack. There's usually a killer or some kind of monster running around loose. That adds to the fun.

This was real life — my own and no movie. I wanted a place to sleep for the night. I also wanted to be able to wake up the next morning still in one piece.

It was nearly midnight. I'd had a rough night so far and I wanted to bed down. Tomorrow I might luck out and all would be well. Meanwhile I was wondering how to find Dr. Stein before he forgot all about me.

There was a long upper landing running high across the big front room. Maybe Dr. Stein is up there fixing up the spare room for you, I told myself.

I went up the stone steps. I counted twenty-two of them. There were doors all along the landing. Like a hotel. I tried the first door. It creaked and opened for me.

It was a bedroom, very dark and dusty, with white covers over the furniture and wall-to-wall cobwebs. Forget this, I told myself. Even Dracula would turn it down. I closed the door.

The next door was locked. For some reason, I felt relieved. If I couldn't get in, I wouldn't get scared. The next door opened easily, no creaks. Before I could look it over, I saw bones on the floor. I closed that door fast. I noticed my heart was thumping. Cool it, I said to myself. Those could be chicken bones.

Only that chicken would have had to be about six feet tall!

If I was a detective, I would have gone back in, sat down with those bones, looked them over and measured them. I'm glad to say, I am no detective.

There were a lot more doors, all closed. If Dr. Stein was in any of them, fixing it up for me, I should have heard him moving around.

I decided to try for him with my voice.

"Dr. Stein!" I called. The place was so big and empty, I got back an echo.

Then I heard something else. A sound that went right through my bones, raising my goose bumps. It was that weird howling sound I heard outside.

"Oh-ooooooooooh-ahhhh!"

I wasn't sure before, but I knew better now. It was coming from inside this house. It seemed to come from below, but the sound floated all around me. If it wasn't a wolf, it was the nearest thing to it.

I couldn't think what that was.

7

The eerie wail stopped so suddenly, I began to think I hadn't heard it at all. Maybe it's only your imagination, I told myself. You're letting yourself get all spooked out.

But I also knew my hearing was always pretty good. If I heard something, it was there. It didn't have to be a wolf. Why would Dr. Stein keep a wolf around. It could have been a dog, I told myself. Dogs sound like that.

That takes care of those bones in the room, too, I told myself. Dogs eat bones.

That kind of cool thinking made me feel better. I decided to forget about checking out the rest of the rooms up there. Instead, I headed down the steps to look for Dr. Stein.

I dribbled my ball down the twenty-two steps, went up and down with a few, making nice moves. Then the ball hit the hard corner of a step and caromed off. I went after it but it took a couple of weird bounces off some more steps and kicked off the main floor into another room.

I ran across the stone floor to get it. I got it and another shocker at the same time. I guess this was the dining room. There was a long table with about fifty chairs around it. I felt eyes watching me. I didn't need this trip, I told myself.

I whipped around. There were a lot of eyes, but they were all on pictures — big oil paintings. I turned from one to the other, puzzled. They all seemed to be the same dude. Black hair, black eyes, black beard. And they all looked exactly like Dr. Stein!

I felt weird, all of a sudden. I knew where I was now. It was a movie I had seen on late TV a couple of hundred times. It's got these two dopey detectives in it, and it's set inside an old castle, like the one I was in now.

They're trying to solve a mystery, or save a girl, and this creepy monster keeps showing up, and they keep bumping into him and nearly dying from fright. The monster comes with the castle, I remembered. The pictures on the walls in the TV movie were weird, too. The eyes moved.

I looked real close at these paintings to see if some joker was behind them looking at me. I heard a loud voice and nearly jumped out of my pants.

"Ah! There you are! I was looking for you!"

It wasn't anything worse than Dr. Stein.

He waved his hands at the pictures. "So you have found my family, I see. I am the last in the line of Steins."

I remembered he had a little boy, but maybe he forgot. "They all — you all look alike, doc," I said.

He nodded, smiling, and introduced me to all his relatives. They were his cousins, uncles, brothers, father, grandfather, and great-grandfather. They were all called Gustave or Otto or Herman.

They all looked the same but the differences were what they wore. A few had uniforms. A couple were standing, holding onto their swords. There weren't any women, unless they were wearing black beards, too.

Dr. Stein pointed his finger to the paintings. "All the Steins have been famous," he said. "Great inventors, doctors, scientists."

"No kidding," I said. "Like what did they do?"

He waved his hand to one on the left. "My great-grandfather Otto invented the wheel. Perhaps you heard about that."

I didn't want to tell the man that the way I heard it, it all happened a long time ago. Way before his great-grandpa Otto. "Yeah," I said. "That was a good one."

He bowed to another picture. "Uncle Herman discovered gravity."

"Hey, man. Terrific," I said.

"My cousin Gustave there made the electric light," he said.

I nodded, not wanting to break the bad news about Edison. "Wow!" I said. "That's some family, all right." I looked at him hoping he wasn't going to tell me he invented salt and pepper. "How about yourself?" I said.

He tapped his puffed-out chest and bowed. "I will be the greatest of them all. You cannot guess what I am working on."

"I hope it's not going to be on relativity," I said.

He shook his head, frowning. "No, no. My cousin Von did that one already." I didn't want to put him down. It was his house, and I needed the night's sleep. He must have read my mind. "Come along," he said. "Your room is ready."

"Great," I said. "I can use it."

"You have finished eating?"

"All I could eat. Thanks a lot, man."

He turned and hurried away before I could ask him who made all that food. I also wondered how come there was so much of it. Those pots were so big, you would have a hard time getting out if you fell in.

I followed him around a bend to another wing of the house. He took out a key, and pushed open a door. "I hope this is all right for you, my boy," he said.

I stared. It was neat and clean. There was a big bed and a carpet on the floor. A basin of water was on top of the dresser. There were no bones, no cobwebs and no snakes coming down off the ceiling.

"Terrific," I said. "This is real neat."

He gave me his funny jerky bow. "Enjoy your night's sleep, Jack. I must go out now. I see you in the morning."

He closed the door behind him softly. I was dead beat, undressed fast, and got under the covers. The sheets were cold but clean. The heavy covers warmed me up.

I was nearly asleep when I wondered why Dr. Stein was so trusting. I could have done a ripoff on him. I went to the door. It was locked from the outside. I shrugged. It's okay, I told myself. Maybe he doesn't want you walking around at night, falling down some stairs.

I sank back into my bed and pillow. I was feeling better. My belly was full and I had a good clean bed for the night. Tomorrow I would think some more about the Glop Oil lady. Before I knew it I was asleep.

I was into a happy dream, driving a hot rod on a drag strip. Then the engine began to conk out on me. Instead of buzzing nice and even, it began to growl. Come on, I told it, cars don't growl. It growled louder. I woke up mad at the dumb car, heard the growling sound, and forgot I was mad. It was easier to be scared. The growling noise filled the room.

I sat up in bed. It sounded like a big dog or cat — or maybe a king-size rat. Whatever it was, I was shaking under the covers, hoping it would go away.

I got my wish and it stopped. Then it came again, this time sounding more like a howl.

It was the same *ow-ooooooh* sound I heard upstairs and the same wolf call outside when Dr. Stein drove me up to the castle. He had told me there were wolves around.

It seemed to me that maybe Dr. Stein was too good-hearted. Maybe he had invited the wolf into his house, too, to spend the night.

Because the sound was coming right out of the wall.

Next door!

8

It seemed like a good idea to get out of the room. Then I remembered Dr. Stein had locked the door. I got out of bed to check it again. It was still locked and I couldn't shake the big heavy door.

Well, I thought, if I can't get out, whatever is next door can't get in. Slowly the howling stopped. I stayed put, trying to sleep with one eye and ear open.

I jerked up again at some new sounds. They were moans and grunts instead of growls. There was a crazy tooth-chattering sound. It didn't sound like a wolf anymore. Maybe more like a gorilla.

Which is worse, I asked myself, a wolf or a gorilla?

Whatever was next door kept it up. The good news, I told myself, is that it's no wolf. The bad news is that it doesn't sound human, either.

I began to wonder what kind of doctor Dr. Stein was.

I remembered his telling me he was working on the greatest invention of all time. He said it wasn't finished yet.

Maybe what was next door was what he was working on — a fright machine! It was doing a good job on me.

Then there were all the things he said his family had invented. He didn't know the stuff had been done long ago by other people.

I began getting a weird feeling that Dr. Stein was some kind of nut. He was like the mad scientist in the sci-fi stories, or the old flicks you see on TV.

He said he had to go out somewhere. I remembered the long wooden box in the back of his pickup truck. Now that I thought of it, it looked like a coffin. Where was he now? Maybe he was digging up a graveyard or burying somebody.

Maybe another hitchhiker took one ride too many. He picked them up and took them to his house. He fed them well and gave them a room for the night.

Then he fed them the next day to the thing next door!

No need to be dumber than you are, I told myself. Let's get out of here.

I dressed in a hurry. The thing next door began making mad, snarling sounds. I hoped I wouldn't see something come out of that wall.

The front wall was covered by a heavy curtain. I pulled it back looking for the window. It was there, a narrow opening high on the wall. Too high for me to reach.

You could do it easy, I told myself, if you were a pole vaulter with a long pole.

I saw that I had two chances. Either I could bounce high off the bed, or I could move the dresser over to the wall and step off that.

I liked the idea of bouncing off the bed and sailing out the window. It would be like Dr. J. floating high in the air until he's ready to stuff the ball into the basket. But the bed was too risky because I had to hold my ball and get through that narrow window up there.

I pushed the dresser closer and climbed up. I forgot all about the basin of water. My foot hit it, and knocked it off. It crashed and splashed into the wall. It woke up the thing which began to howl louder than ever. "I'm going, I'm going," I told it.

I reached up for the window and got another surprise. It was just an opening, no glass. Instead it had iron bars and wood shutters. It looked as if Dr. Stein didn't like to lose his overnight guests.

The bars were pretty close together, but fear made me thinner. I got the shutters back and crawled through. My ball barely made it.

When I got to the outside wall, I looked

down. All I saw was blackness. I didn't see any yellow eyes or hear wolves. Because of the ball, I couldn't hold on long to the iron bars. I pushed off and let go.

I thought it would be only a little fall because my room was on the main floor, but I kept dropping and dropping. It seemed like I was going to be in a free fall forever.

Then my feet hit something hard. At the same time, I felt a big splash. Suddenly I was going down in water over my head. I kept trying to remember not to breathe.

9

When I popped to the surface, I began to swim. There was a lot of water going two ways. At first, I thought I'd fallen into a ditch. Then I remembered about castles and the moats. The moat is the water that is kept around the castle to keep out invaders. The way into the castle was over a drawbridge.

When Dr. Stein brought me to his castle, he drove over the bridge. I thought it was just more of the same narrow road or part of his driveway. Now that I knew better, I still had the problem of getting out of the moat.

The water was deep and the sides were high. My ball helped me float in the water, but the sides were too high for me to climb out.

I decided to keep swimming. I wanted to see what was on the other side. When I got there, it was the same. There was still plenty of water and a high bank way over my head. It was like my own private swimming pool. I could swim all night with nobody bothering me.

You can also drown here, I reminded myself.

When you're in the water, and can't get out, and think about drowning, you call for help. So I did that. I did some more swimming, and a lot of yelling.

I felt like a real jerk. Here I was making nearly as much noise myself as that thing inside the castle that made me jump out.

I saw light flash on the castle walls. I stopped yelling and listened. There was the sound of a car. Maybe it's those two bad dudes, Alphonse and Gaston, I told myself. They're going to drive off the bridge and then we can all drown together.

The car came closer and stopped. I yelled some more. A flashlight was shining on my face. All I could see was the light.

Then I heard a voice I knew. "Jack, is that you down there?"

That makes twice he's saving your life, I told myself.

"Hi, Dr. Stein," I said. "Can you get me out?"

He threw down a thick rope. I grabbed hold and he pulled. I got to the top of the bank and sat down.

"How did you get down into the moat, Jack?" Dr. Stein asked.

"I fell out the window," I said.

10

I was cold and wet. I didn't argue about going back inside. Dr. Stein gave me a bathrobe and I hung up my wet clothes to dry in front of a fireplace.

There wasn't a sound from the thing that was howling and growling before. The fire felt so warm and good, I fell asleep watching it.

When I woke up, it was morning. There was a blanket over me. Dr. Stein was a good guy keeping me warm. He never said a word about why I left. And I didn't tell him anything about what was happening next door. Maybe I would have but I fell asleep first.

He wasn't around when I woke up. The castle was quiet. Okay, I told myself, you had enough. Let's move it.

I dressed fast. I didn't want to think about breakfast. All I wanted was to get out. I had to get back on the road and away from this weird castle. I had to find my way back to Paris and the Glop Oil lady. It was time to get everything straight.

Nobody was guarding the front door. All I had to do was walk out. I stepped softly. There was no need to wake up anybody. My hand touched the door knob.

It froze there.

My mind was going way ahead. I was back in the states, back in Los Angeles, at home with my family. And I was telling the kid sister Susie all about the weird trip to Paris.

So she says right off, "Well, what *was* that thing next door?"

I looked at her and shrugged. "I never found out, sis. I split. I had to get back to Paris."

She was looking at me, seeing right through me. "You what?"

"Well, you know, I had to get this whole thing cleared up. About the pot which was the cake and so on."

She shakes her head, not believing me. "This man, this Dr. Stein, he tells you he has created the world's greatest new thing. You think you hear it from the next room. And you mean to tell me you leave without looking at it, seeing what it is?"

"I guess so," I said.

Her voice is down. "I hate to have a brother who is chicken," he says.

So I am at the front door, thinking about this, seeing the whole scene in my head, clear as anything, as though it is really happening.

And I know now I can't go out that front door — not yet, anyway.

The thing to do was to ask Dr. Stein about it. He could say yes or no. After all, he found me on the road, took me home, fixed my cuts, fed me, and gave me the bed for the night.

If I walk out, the kid sister is going to call me other names besides chicken. One of them is rat fink.

I heard a door closing. Dr. Stein was coming my way. "Good morning, young man," he said. "I hope you slept well."

I nodded. "This time it was better." I pointed to the door. "What's in that room there?"

He looked. "That's the room next to yours, Jack."

"I know," I said. "What's in there? It scared me silly."

He stared. "What do you mean?"

"All night long there was this howling. I thought it was a wolf. Then it made other noises."

He cocked his head, as if listening. "What kind of noises?"

"Like moans and groans. Real weird sounds. Like there was some kind of monster in there."

"Perhaps you were dreaming," he said.

I shook my head. "No way, man. Those sounds kept me awake."

He looked at his watch. "Breakfast is ready, Jack. Perhaps after you eat, you will feel better."

"Okay," I said. "But then, I have to be going, you know."

He shrugged, taking my arm. "Come. We will talk about it."

I decided it wouldn't hurt to eat first.

11

The kitchen table was loaded. There was oatmeal, eggs, bread, fruit, and milk. The pots were still cooking on the stove.

"Hey, who does all the cooking here?" I said.

Dr. Stein smiled. "I have a housekeeper, my boy."

I looked around. "So far, I haven't seen anybody."

"Perhaps there are too many rooms here," he said. He pointed at the plates. "Eat up Jack. You must be hungry."

I ate my share and more. Dr. Stein took some fruit and coffee. He lit his pipe, and looked at his watch.

"Thanks for the food and the night's sleep, doc," I said. "I have to go now. Maybe I can hitch a ride back."

He waved his pipe. "Where can you go?

You told me the police and the customs people were looking for you."

"Maybe things are cool now. Maybe the Glop Oil lady talked them out of it. They still owe me the free week in Paris."

He shook his head. "If they do not believe your story, what then? What can you do? It may not yet be safe for you there."

"Maybe. But I took off before knowing what they were going to do with me. Maybe I can find Alphonse and Gaston back in Paris. I'll work out some kind of a deal."

"Paris is a big city to find someone," he said. "You do not even know where to find this Glop Oil lady."

I went through my pockets. "I had it written down somewhere," I said. "Now I can't find the name of the hotel where I was supposed to be staying."

"You can stay here," Dr. Stein said. "Perhaps you can take care of Frank when I'm not here."

"You mean baby-sit?" Maybe I could make a few dollars hanging around until I got things cleared up.

Dr. Stein nodded. "He does not like to be alone."

"Well, maybe," I said. "Only I can't stay too long, you know. I have to be getting back."

A low humming sound began coming from one of the back rooms. It got louder and sounded more like moaning. Then it got real loud, an awful howling sound. I looked at Dr. Stein. He kept puffing away on his pipe, as if he didn't hear anything.

I pointed over his shoulder. "Hey, that's the same noise I heard last night."

"What?" he said.

I wondered suddenly if Dr. Stein was a vet, an animal doctor. "Don't you hear that? It sounds like some kind of wolf or big dog."

He smiled, shaking his head. "No, no, you are mistaken, my boy."

The howls changed to sounds like groans and moans. Dr. Stein looked at his watch. The groans and moans became wails.

"Maybe you have somebody sick back there? A patient coming down from drugs?"

He shook his head. "What are you talking about? There is no one sick here."

I could hardly hear his voice over the noise back there. "Then what's all that about?" I said. "All those sounds."

Dr. Stein looked at me. He put down his pipe. "I suppose I can tell you. But it is a great secret. You will be the first to know."

"Well, okay," I said, "if you think you can trust me."

He shrugged. "Remember I told you I was working on a great new discovery?" I nodded, wondering what weird thing he was going to tell me next. He wagged his thumb over his shoulder to the howling noise. "That is it, Jack. The greatest invention in the history of the world."

"Okay," I said nervously, "what is it, some new kind of hi-fi tuner?"

He stared. "What is hi-fi?" He tapped his chest. "I have taken a dead soul and given it life. I have made a new human being."

I stared at him. "You what?"

The din got louder. It was sounding like a howling wolf, sometimes like a hungry lion. The sounds kept coming. Dr. Stein looked at his timer again. For the first time, he looked a little put out about it.

He put down his pipe. "Perhaps he needs something. Come along, Jack. You will see for yourself." Another long howl from back there made him start to run. "Frank," he called, "Papa is coming."

I followed him. I was holding my ball, not dribbling it. My knees felt weak. Frank was the name of his little baby, the one he said was three months old.

It would take about three hundred three-month-old kids to make all that noise, I was thinking. And I never heard of any kids doing that kind of howling. Wolf Boy was the only one I could think of. I was about to change my mind about taking this look at Frank. I didn't have to see everything.

But Dr. Stein came back, grabbed my arm, and hurried me along. "You came here just in time, Jack. Frank will be happy to see you. Perhaps he has been kept alone too long."

I went along, trying to be cool and not scared. I was hoping this wasn't feeding time for whatever was in there. Praying he wasn't hungry.

"What did you make him out of?" I said.

"Spare parts," said Dr. Stein.

12

We went back to the sounds coming from the room. Dr. Stein stopped at the door. He rapped on it. "Papa is coming, Frank," he called. "Everything is all right."

The howling stopped. "You see, he knows my voice," Dr. Stein said. He took a big key ring off the wall. There was a large padlock on the door and he snapped it open with one of the big iron keys.

It was quiet inside when he opened the door, and dark, too. I was hoping that whatever came out to eat me would try the ball first.

Dr. Stein flipped some wall switches. Lights sputtered on slowly. I held my breath wondering what I was going to see.

It was a big room with a skylight high overhead. There were cabinets all along the walls. A lot of dials glowed with colored lights and switches. In the center of the room was a long table. On it was lying a body so big it would have dwarfed any player in the National Basketball Association. It was partly covered with a sheet and lying awfully still.

Something about it made my hair stand on end, gave me goose bumps. I knew I had seen it somewhere before!

"Frankenstein!" I said.

Dr. Stein looked at me. "What?"

I pointed to the huge figure on the table. "Frankenstein's monster. Dr. Frankenstein made it."

Dr. Stein looked angry. "What are you talking about? I am Dr. Stein. *I* made it."

I had to tell him before the world told him. "No, honest, doc. You're too late. It's already been done. First, it was a book, then a movie. You see it a lot in the old movies on TV. It's Frankenstein meets the Wolfman and all that stuff."

He shook his head. He looked worried. "You are telling me the truth, Jack? Some other Stein made Frank?"

"Well, not the same one. Not this one, anyway." I stole a quick look at the giant lying there. He looked as if he were asleep. The face looked like the old monster I was used to, the kind of face you don't forget.

Dr. Stein was upset now. He tugged at his beard. His eyes were puzzled and staring. "I will be the laughingstock of the world! All the Steins have been the very first. Now I will be only the second."

I didn't have the heart to lay the truth on

him about that, either. "Well, anyway, you did it on your own. You didn't see it on TV, because you never watch it, you said. You didn't copy it from anybody. Besides, who knows? Maybe yours will work out better."

"What do you mean?"

"It was a bad trip, doc. The monster got away. It scared the townspeople. So they all came around and trapped it in the old mill. They burned it down."

Dr. Stein came close to the big hulk he called Frank. He began patting him on the head. "How could they do such a terrible thing? See how gentle my Frank is. He will not hurt anyone. As soon as I find the right brain for him, he will be perfect."

Well, it was his baby. "Good deal," I said. Frank looked big and strong enough to tear down the castle stone by stone. But if Dr. Stein said he was gentle, it was okay with me.

"He is perfect all over," Dr. Stein yelled. His hand slapped the giant's chest which made a sound like a big drum. "Perhaps that other doctor did not do such a good job. You will not see my Frank turned into some sort of freak from a circus."

It looked like all that slapping and pounding was waking Frank up. No sooner had Dr. Stein said the last word, when Frank's eyes opened.

Dr. Stein patted his head. "It is all right, Frank. Papa is here. No one will hurt you. You are the strongest man in the world."

Frank smiled. One big arm went up. His hand went to his head. He groaned. *"Oh-h-h!"*

Dr. Stein clapped his hands, excited. "Did you hear? He spoke!"

I heard. Now he began to sit up. The belts holding him on the table snapped off. I froze, watching him brush them away.

Dr. Stein waved his hands. "Wait, Frank! You must not move. You are not finished yet. Be a good boy and lie down again."

Frank wasn't paying attention. His legs swung up and he sat up. His legs looked stiff as he put his feet on the floor. Dr. Stein stopped to pick up the broken straps.

"Help me, Jack," he said to me. "We must put him down again."

My eyes bugged at Frank getting up. He swayed on his feet. He was bigger than Wilt. He was bigger than Kareem, Dawkins or Caldwell Jones. He was bigger than any of the giants who play basketball. He looked at least seven-foot-five and had to weigh over three hundred pounds.

Dr. Stein tripped over the strap and fell. "Stop him, Jack," he said.

I looked at Frank again. No way, I thought. He's got to be kidding. I froze against the wall near the doorway, hoping I was invisible. I held my ball against my chest. My heart was going *thump thump thump*.

Frank came on, walking as if he had stiff knees or a charley horse. *Clump clump. Shuffle shuffle.* Like that. His eyes were yellow. They were staring on ahead toward the open door. Then he saw me and stopped.

His shoulders swung around. They looked as wide as a door. His arms dangled loosely at his sides. Then he saw the ball. His eyes lit up. I could swear he smiled. His big head wagged from side to side.

Then he raised his arms. I looked up, trying to back some more of me into the wall. His hands reached out, palms up. They looked as big as shovels.

I knew what he wanted.

My ball!

13

I froze to the wall trying not to die of fright. His big hands beckoned in a "gimme" gesture. His eyes were pleading.

I found my voice although I didn't recognize it was me speaking. "Do you want the ball?" I said.

He wore a goofy smile. His head bobbed up and down. I was wondering how to tell him it was the only ball I had. That I never gave it to anybody. That me and that ball had done a lot of time together. Grown up together.

Dr. Stein came running over. His arms were carrying the sheet and the straps. He tripped over them again and went down. "Don't go, Frank!" he cried. "Don't let him go out, Jack. He'll hurt himself."

The big guy turned his head at all the noise. Somehow it was what I wanted him to do. Before I knew what I was doing, I was bouncing my ball, moving with it, shifting from side to side.

Frank turned back. He followed every move. I began a slow dribble. *Bam bam, bounce bounce*. Then I was backing out of the doorway with it. Frank was so interested, he followed me.

He came on, grunting with every step. He had his eyes on the ball as if he was hypnotized. His big head was going up and down as he followed each bounce. His arms stretched out trying to get at the ball.

He followed me out to the main hall. I kept some space between us. It was as if I was in a big game now, one-on-one against the biggest power forward to be found. It was the first chance I ever had to be up against one of the real big guys.

It didn't matter that he didn't know basketball. He had the main idea in his eyes. Get the ball. There was only one thing wrong with this make-believe game. I didn't know what Frank would do to get the ball.

Out of the corner of my eye, I saw Dr. Stein standing in the doorway of the lab. He was yelling, waving at me. He wanted me to bring Frank back, I guess. Only I didn't know how to do that.

I kept going back until I felt the wall behind me. Then I was in a pocket and had to get out. I looked up at Frank to check his temper. He wasn't mad. He just followed the ball with his eyes, tracing every move I made. He never let me get too far away, or out of reach, I noticed.

In a game, I would have to drive around him to shoot for my basket. I would jump for my lay-up. He wouldn't be allowed to touch me. He would have to back up or draw a foul.

But Frank didn't know any basketball rules. There was no way I could power past him, or muscle my way through like the big guys do.

There was nobody there to pass it off to. I kept on bouncing the ball and Frank kept coming closer and closer. He was reaching out with his long arms, trying now to swat the ball away with those big hands.

I decided to get him off me by shooting over his head. There was no basket there, but I thought if I got the ball in the air, I could run around him. I could get it back while he was turning to follow it.

I shot the moon ball. It was over his head. It seemed to be the perfect move.

Only one thing was wrong. I didn't figure how big Frank was. His eyes moved with the ball. His body went up. His arms seemed to reach to the ceiling. And when they came down, he was holding the ball.

He didn't eat it. He didn't knock me down for giving him such a hard time. Instead he grinned happily, and began to bounce the ball on the floor the way I had. He kept bouncing it, catching it, moving back with it, acting like any guy who knew what to do with a basketball.

He kept moving back. He bounced and dribbled the ball as if he had found a new toy. I couldn't blame him. I liked it, too.

His back hit the front door and he stopped. Then he turned around, holding the ball. He opened the door and walked out. The door slammed shut behind him.

Dr. Stein came running over. He grabbed my arm. "This is terrible," he said. "He should not be outside by himself. Come along, Jack. We must stop him. We will bring him back here."

I didn't know how we were going to do that. But Frank had my ball. I let Dr. Stein talk me into it. I didn't know if he was waiting outside for us. I let Dr. Stein go out first. After all, it was his baby.

14

We jumped into the car and set out after Frank. It didn't take long before we saw him. He was in the middle of the narrow road. He was moving from side to side, bouncing my ball. From where I sat, next to Dr. Stein, it looked as if he was dribbling it.

"Hey, doc," I said, "Frankie handles that ball pretty well. With his size, you know, he can make a pretty good basketball player."

"What are you talking about?" Dr. Stein said. "He is not finished yet. He doesn't know his own name. He is still without a brain. How can he play this basketball?"

"Well, they make a lot of money," I said. "Some dudes make a million bucks a year at it."

Dr. Stein nearly drove off the road. "A million dollars, did you say, Jack?"

"That or close to it," I said. "They get contracts that pay a couple of million for only a few years. It's a big sport."

"So much money," Dr. Stein said, "for playing with a ball?"

"Well, you have to be good at it, too, doc," I said.

He shrugged. "We talk about it after we get Frank back. Then I must finish my work on him."

I looked at Frank down the road, walking, and bouncing my ball. "He looks okay to me."

Dr. Stein shook his head. "He still needs the brain. It is important to find the right one for him." He suddenly laughed. "Maybe I find somebody who has this basketball brain you talk about. Then we try to make the transfer."

I wondered about that. If he was thinking what I was thinking, I didn't like the idea. Frank had my ball. No way he was going to get my brain, too. You have to get out of here, I told myself. Find that Glop Oil lady and do what you were supposed to do.

Dr. Stein was driving slowly behind Frank. We were close to him when he suddenly realized a car was behind him. He turned his head. He saw us but didn't see the ditch alongside the road. He turned his ankle and went down with a big crash. He hit his head on a big rock.

Dr. Stein braked. I saw Frank out cold. I jumped out to get my ball. By the time I got the ball and came back, Dr. Stein was kneeling beside Frank, looking him over.

"You will be all right, Frank," he said. "Papa is here."

Frank opened his eyes. "Who are you?" he said.

Dr. Stein said, "I am your papa, Frank. Dr. Stein. When did you learn to talk?"

Frank rubbed his head. "Are you kidding, doc? I always knew how to talk."

"But you have been with me a long time, Frank. You never said a word from the day I found you."

Frank sat up. "You must be nuts. I don't know you." He looked around and saw me. "Where did they go?" he said.

"Who?" I said.

"The circus," Frank said.

"What circus is that, Frank?" Dr. Stein said.

"The one I work for."

"You work for a circus? What do you do there?"

Frank lifted his hand. He picked Dr. Stein up with it and held him up in the air. "What do you think? I'm the circus strongman."

15

Dr. Stein spun slowly in Frank's hand. He didn't look like he was enjoying it. "Put me down, Frank," he said. "We will talk about it."

Seeing how easily Frank lifted him, and hearing him speak, made me wonder who was crazy now. "He talks okay," I said to Dr. Stein. "Maybe he has a brain after all."

Frank looked at me. "Who says I don't?" he growled.

Dr. Stein was shaking his head. "I don't understand this. When I found you at the bottom of the mountain, you were dead. It was I who gave you a new life."

"How did you do that?" Frank asked.

Dr. Stein drew himself up, tapping his chest. "I am a great doctor, Frank. I have been bringing you to life for nearly three months."

I had an idea. "Maybe he didn't die, after

all, doc. Maybe he just hit his head and was knocked out."

Instead of getting angry, Dr. Stein nodded his head. "It happens sometimes that way, Jack. The mind goes, too. We call it amnesia, the loss of memory."

Frank got up. "Three months," he said. "You mean I've been with you for three months?"

Dr. Stein shrugged. "What do you remember last about the mountain?"

Frank looked up to the hills. He pointed to the distance. "We were coming along the mountain road up there. Five wagons. It was night. A wheel came off a wagon. I went out to get it. I stepped over the edge, I guess. Before I knew it, I was falling. That's all I remember, falling and falling." He rubbed the back of his head. "I must have hit my head on a rock. It still hurts."

"Hey, that's how I got here, too," I said. "I was up there when my ball got away. I went after it, and down I went. Dr. Stein found me at the bottom. I thought I was dead, but he showed me I wasn't."

"You were lucky," Dr. Stein said. "Look at what happened to Frank."

"I lost my job at the circus," Frank said. "That's what happened."

"What did you do there as a strongman?" I asked.

Frank moved his big hands. "I bent iron and steel bars. I lifted horses and cows. At every town we stopped, I put on my show. I'm the strongest man in the world."

"What was your name then, Frank," said Dr. Stein.

Frank looked puzzled. He rubbed his head. "I don't remember," he said. "How come you call me Frank?"

Dr. Stein smiled and lifted Frank's sleeve. "Here," he said. "It is tattooed on your arm."

Frank looked at the blue tattoo. "Oh, yeah, I remember I had that done a long time ago."

"Do you remember your last name, Frank?" said Dr. Stein.

Frank lifted his big arms and sighed. "It's the same. Frank Frank. I never use it."

"Why not?" said Dr. Stein.

"It sounds like a dog barking," Frank said.

16

Dr. Stein began to cry. "I have lost my little boy. Now I have to start all over again."

"Well, doc, me, too," Frank said. "I'm out of my job. I have to look for my circus." He began to pump his arms and flex his muscles. He tried a few knee bends. "I don't know if I can hack it now. I feel stiff. Out of shape."

"It's the spare parts," I told him.

Frank stared down at me. "What spare parts?" he said in a deep, rumbling growl.

I turned to Dr. Stein. "Maybe you ought to tell him what's his and what's yours. So he doesn't break anything."

Frank stopped in the middle of a stretch. "What are you talking about?" He thumped his big chest. "This is still me."

Dr. Stein cleared his throat. His eyes didn't look too happy. "Well, Frank, my boy," he said. "I had to make a few changes, you know."

Frank stared at him. "Like what?" he growled.

Dr. Stein waved his hands. "You were all banged up, Frank. Your legs were broken. I made you new legs."

"How did you do that?" Frank said.

"Shin splints," said Dr. Stein. "I put steel bars all around to support your bones."

Frank bent over to look at his legs. He lifted them one at a time. "No wonder they feel stiff and heavy." He stamped his foot. "They weigh a ton."

"Then there was your neck," Dr. Stein said. "That was also broken. I mixed some cement. I made a collar for you to support your head."

Frank touched his neck. His eyes rolled. "Cement? How come cement?"

Dr. Stein shrugged. "The light was bad. I meant to use plaster of Paris. I picked the wrong bag. It was a simple mistake, Frank."

"Yeah," Frank said.

"By the time I found out, it had set hard as stone, Frank," Dr. Stein said.

Frank tried to turn his head. "Ow!" he said, "Cement is for steps and driveways, doc."

"Anyway your head did not fall off, so it worked out all right," said Dr. Stein. "But doing your face used my very best talents. I did not know what you were supposed to look like. So I put on pieces of this and that until you looked like someone again, Frank."

Frank put his hand to his nose. Then to his

cheeks. He felt all over his face. "Hey, I don't feel anything. What do I look like now, doc?"

Dr. Stein lifted his hands. "There is a mirror on the side of the car, Frank. See for yourself."

Frank stiffly walked over to the mirror of the pickup. He looked into it. "Oh, no," he said. "Frankenstein!"

"That's strange," Dr. Stein said. "Jack here said the same thing when he saw you."

Frank kept staring at his reflection in the mirror. He felt his forehead, the top of his head. "Terrific," he said slowly. "You made me look like Dr. Frankenstein's monster."

"I never heard of this doctor," said Dr. Stein. "What was his specialty?"

"Scaring people," Frank said. His big head wagged from side to side. "I don't believe this." He looked at me. "Hey, kid. Do I look like what I think I look like?"

"I only saw it in movies," I said. "I never saw it in real life."

"Yeah, I guess," Frank said. "But I'm *him*, right?"

"If not, you're real close," I said.

Frank sat down on the big rock he had hit his head on. "I don't know if I'm ready for this," he said.

"It is this other doctor's fault," Dr. Stein shouted. "He should have stuck to treating colds and measles."

Frank was tapping his face, feeling his nose and forehead. "If my dear old mother saw me now, she would drop dead."

Dr. Stein came over to him. "You must remember, Frank," he said, "I thought you were dead. Remember, I gave you a new life."

"Yeah," Frank said. "What a life this is going to be."

"It will be all right, Frank," Dr. Stein said. "We will find your circus and get you your old job back as strongman. Then you will be happy again."

Frank slowly shook his head from side to side. "No way, doc. The only job that circus will give me now is as the star of the freak show."

"Hey, I have an idea," I said.

Frank looked at me. "I have one, too," he said gloomily. "My idea is to break Dr. Stein into little pieces. But I'll hear yours first."

"Take your time, Jack," Dr. Stein said. "There is no hurry."

17

"For one thing," I said, "you'd be crazy to take the job in a freak show. Even if they gave it to you."

Frank shrugged his big shoulders. "Maybe I would. But I need the job. I have to eat, don't I?"

"How much would they pay you?" I said.

He didn't have to think long about it. "Not much. Peanuts."

"That's why you'd be crazy to take it," I said. "I know a way you can make a million dollars a year."

"I know that way, too," Frank said. "But I have no reason to be robbing banks."

I held up my ball, spinning it on my finger. "You can get it the honest way," I said. "Playing with this."

"Basketball?" Frank asked.

He surprised me. "You know about the game?" I said.

"Well, sure," Frank said. "Just because I worked in a circus doesn't make me a dummy. Also I played some ball in school."

"Where was that?"

"Back in the United States." He grinned. "I was born there. New Jersey. My father was American, my mother French. After he died, she came back home, taking me with her. But I was getting too big for school then, and got jobs using my muscles until I joined the circus full time."

"Okay, so you know basketball and how much the stars make," I said.

Frank held up his big hand. "Hold it. Years back, when I still was in school, they weren't making that much money."

"It's different now," I said. "With guys like Kareem, and Doctor J, and Bird and Magic — they really make a lot of bread."

"Well, I don't know," Frank said. "I've seen it played. The guys move around a lot. I'm too slow. I'm big and strong, but I can't move fast enough to get out of my own way."

"Sure you can. All you have to do is start working out. Get yourself back in shape."

Frank stood testing his legs. "How can I play a game where you run around?" he said. "I'm stiff. I can't move too well. They'll laugh at me."

"That's because of all the stuff Dr. Stein laid on you, Frank," I said. "Your bones must have healed by now. Inside, you're okay. You're still strong. Once you get that collar off your neck and the iron braces off your legs, you'll feel better."

"Do you think so?" he said.

"I'm pretty sure," I said. "You'll be a hundred pounds lighter."

Frank stood thinking about it. He lifted his hand and hit a terrific karate chop on the back of his neck. There was a cracking sound. He did it again on the other side. The cement came loose, cracking into small pieces. Frank brushed it all away and turned his head, looking happy. "Hey, how about that?" he said.

"Maybe you can do something about your legs now," I said. "Then we can get going."

Frank rolled up his pants leg. There were iron bars from his knees to his shoes. He bent and pulled. The iron bent. Frank kept pulling. The iron broke off. He did this a few more times, and his left leg was free.

He bent to the other side. The bars began to bend like spaghetti. He put on more pressure. All the bars fell off.

Frank lifted his legs. He began to dance around like a kid. "Hey, look," he yelled. "I can do this." He began to do knee bends, but fell down. He looked at me. "What happened?"

"I guess you've been laid up too long. You're a little out of shape, Frank."

"It takes time," Dr. Stein said. "You will have to train your body all over again to do what you want it to do."

Frank nodded, rubbing his legs. "Yeah, I guess."

"Meanwhile," I said, "you can think about playing basketball for a living. You might like it."

Frank shrugged. "Well, it sounds okay. I don't know if I can do it, but it might be worth trying."

I bounced my ball. "You'll see. The rim is ten feet high. You're so big, all you'd have to do is reach up and stuff the ball in."

Frank smiled. It was kind of weird seeing somebody who looked like Frankenstein's monster smiling. I could see that if Frank ever got into the game, lots of players would be getting heart attacks when he came on the floor.

Frank pointed to my ball. "Okay. You have the ball. How soon do we get started?"

"Well, first I have to find my Glop Oil lady," I said.

Frank looked at me blankly. "What's that all about?"

I told him the story — about the contest the kid sister won — my taking the trip for her — the bad dude at the airport — the cake for his old mom that was pot — and Alphonse and Gaston. "If I don't get back to that Orly airport, and Paris, and the Glop lady, I'm in trouble with the law. And when I get there, I'll be in worse trouble if I can't get them to think I'm innocent."

"So what are you doing here?" Frank asked.

I explained about my falling off the mountain, just as he had, after Alphonse and Gaston faked me out. I told him how Dr. Stein found me and took me to his home.

"Hey, you're lucky you didn't break anything," Frank said. "Otherwise I'd have a monster kid brother."

"Nonsense," Dr. Stein said. "I never make the same mistake twice. Anyway, I think Frank looks very nice. At least he looks different from everyone else."

Frank groaned. "You can say that again, doc."

"If you make good in basketball, Frank," I said, "you can have yourself done over by a plastic surgeon. That kind of doc could take off the face Dr. Stein gave you and make you another one. Any kind you want."

"That will cost plenty," Frank said.

"When you make a million bucks a year, Frank, you can buy a new face for every day of the week," I told him. What I didn't want to tell Frank was that if he ever got into the National Basketball Association, his face and all, looking like Frankenstein's monster would make him a big draw.

Frank looked at Dr. Stein. "Is that right, doc? Can I have another face built on top of the one you gave me?"

Dr. Stein laughed. "Of course, my boy. I am just a poor country doctor. If I did such a marvelous job, just think how much better a real plastic doctor can make you look. Only it will cost much money, Frank."

Big Frank rubbed his hands together. "If I become a big basketball star, doc, I can afford it. With that kind of money, I can get the best doctor money can buy."

"Well, it's not just the money, Frank," I said.

"It's not?"

"No," I said. "The thing is to find a doctor who never saw any fright movies on TV."

"That's for sure," Frank said.

18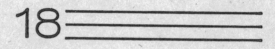

We were back on the road again, riding in Dr. Stein's pickup. He decided he owed it to Frank to help him get started in a new life. "It was my own fault," Dr. Stein said. "I kept him tied down to my table. How did I know he was alive?"

I remembered all the food in those pots in the kitchen. "Well, he was still eating," I said. "How did you figure that?"

Dr. Stein tapped his head. "I thought that if he kept eating, when I brought him back to life, he would be strong and healthy."

"I heard that when you're dead, you lose your appetite," I said.

"I know that, too," Dr. Stein said. "That's what made Frank such an interesting case."

19

Frank was too big to fit in the cab of the pickup. He had to sit in the open back. I joined him there. I was still trying to get him used to the idea of playing basketball for a living.

Frank shrugged his wide shoulders. "Listen, first things first. We will see what we can do for you at the airport. Maybe you took off too soon, and the whole mess is cleared up now. I have the rest of my life to see what I'll do. You only have the week here for your trip. You don't ever want to be in trouble with the law, Jack."

"I don't want to be," I said. "It just happened."

"Well, maybe it will all work out," Frank said.

Dr. Stein was taking us over a nice country road. French farmers were working in the fields. There were chickens, cows and barns. Everything looked really nice. If I knew for sure I wasn't going to be arrested when we got to Orly airport, it would have looked even nicer.

Frank was lying back enjoying the ride. Suddenly he banged on the cab window. "Stop the car! Hold it!" he yelled.

Dr. Stein braked. The pickup skidded to a stop. But Frank was already jumping out of the tailgate.

"Where you going?" I asked.

He pointed toward a barn off the road a bit. "That barn there. Do you see that sign on it?" He kept on running for the barn with his long legs stretched out.

Dr. Stein looked at me. "What is wrong?"

I pointed to Frank. "He saw something there."

Frank was standing at the side of the barn when we got there. He was looking at a faded white poster. When we were close, he put his finger on it. "There, you see? I wasn't making it up. That's me at my old circus job."

It was an old circus poster. The colors were faded, but the words were all there:

~~~~~~~~~~~~~~~~~~~~~~

Coming soon!

MARVEL CIRCUS

SEE THE STRONG MAN

**HE BENDS STEEL BARS
HE LIFTS HORSES
HE CRUSHES STONE**

~~~~~~~~~~~~~~~~~~~~~~

There were pictures on the poster. A big guy with muscles like rocks was lifting a horse over his head. In another picture he was bending an iron bar in half. Then there was one where he was smashing a rock with his fist.

Frank was rubbing his big hands, grinning. "That's how I used to look. Not bad, huh?"

I looked closer. That must have been Frank if he recognized himself. I couldn't say for sure because of his new face. He looked like a big, good-natured guy, then wearing about a ton of muscle.

"I wasn't pretty," Frank said. "But at least I didn't scare anybody." He tore the poster off the boards and began to roll it up. "I'd better keep this. I can show people what I really used to look like."

Somebody was yelling at us. A man came running from the fields. I guess he was the farmer who owned the place. His face was very red. He looked mad. He was yelling something in French.

Frank turned. "Now, wait —"

The angry farmer got a good look at Frank now. His jaw dropped. His red face got white. His eyes bugged out. He gave a loud yell. He took a step back, turned and began to run.

"Hey, wait!" Frank said. "I won't hurt you."

The man kept running, yelling at the top of his lungs. He disappeared behind some trees. We lost him for awhile, and then I saw him running across the distant fields.

Some people were following him. They turned and began coming our way. They were holding long sticks and pitchforks.

"What's that about?" Frank said.

I had a sinking feeling. "Hey, watch it," I said. "That dude and his friends are coming to get us."

Dr. Stein snorted. "Ridiculous. Do not worry. I will explain it to them."

"Do they know you?" Frank said.

"No, but I will say I am your doctor," Dr. Stein said.

Frank looked at me. His eyes looked troubled. "What do you think, Jack?" he said softly.

I didn't like the pitchforks. Also, I had already seen the movie on the monster a lot of times. "We'd better move it," I said. "Those dudes aren't going to listen."

Rocks began to fly through the air. A few came close. We ran for the pickup. Dr. Stein jumped behind the wheel. "I do not understand," he said. "Why are they doing this?"

"They think he's the Frankenstein monster," I said. "You'd better get this heap moving, doc."

He started slowly. Rocks were landing near us. Some were really close. A gun went off. The bullet hit the fender with a pinging sound. It scared Dr. Stein into driving faster.

Frank was holding his head. "This is crazy," he said. "I never hurt anybody in my life."

I forgot about my problem. Frank was the one who really had the problem. He scared those people out of their minds.

He looked at me. "I saw that movie a long time ago, Jack," he said. "Do you remember how it ended?"

"Yeah," I said. "Sorry about that."

"They got him, huh?" he said.

"Well, yes," I said. "But remember, that was only a movie."

"I really look like him, huh?" he said.

"Those people back there thought so," I said.

He wagged his big head slowly. "Gee," Frank said. "That poor guy. I feel sorry for him."

20

Dr. Stein didn't stop again. The narrow country road got wider. There were more houses, more cars, and more people. I began to worry. How would Frank do in the NBA if he scared people? Maybe getting him to play ball wasn't such a hot idea.

Then I began to worry about myself. What was going to happen when we got to Orly? What if the police were waiting for me? They were probably ready to give me a bad time.

"Do not worry, Jack," Dr. Stein said. "Everything will be all right. You and Frank are part of my family now. I will take care of everything."

I kept looking for signs. "I don't see Orly airport," I said.

We were driving over a wide bridge. A big city seemed to be all around us. "I do not drive this way often," Dr. Stein said. "Perhaps I took the wrong road somewhere."

"Maybe we can stop, doc. I'll ask somebody."

Frank pointed ahead. "I know where we are. This is Paris."

"Are you sure?" I said.

"Sure I'm sure," Frank said. "There's only one thing like that in the world. It's only in Paris."

"What is?" I said.

He pointed again. "The Eiffel Tower."

I looked out past his finger. Off in the distance, going way up into the sky, was this huge spider-like thing. It was just like the pictures I had seen of it. Only bigger.

"Terrific," I said. "Now I can tell the kid sister I saw it."

Dr. Stein stopped the pickup. "What is the big hurry for us to go to Orly?" he asked.

I shrugged. "No big hurry, doc. I just want to get it over and done with. I'd like to know how I stand with the law. Maybe I could get on with my Glop Oil trip."

He rubbed his black bushy beard. "Do you know something? I have lived in France all my life. But this is also my first time to see Paris."

"Well," I said, "okay, now you saw it. Let's go."

He shook his head. "It is one time in a lifetime for us, my boy. We take a better look at it. For the Eiffel Tower, the way to see it is from the top."

It was late afternoon. I looked at the reddish-brown girders. "How do we do that?"

Dr. Stein started moving his pickup again. "We start at the bottom."

We got closer. The tower looked even higher. "Hey, it looks like some climb up," I said.

"So we take the elevator," said Dr. Stein.

21

Frank wanted to go up to the top, too. But he was afraid of scaring people. "If they see me," he said, "they will be flying off the top."

"You look very good to me, Frank," said Dr. Stein. "Do not mind what some people think."

"I have a better idea," I said. "All we have to do is cover him up, sort of."

Frank went for that. There was a blanket in the back of the pickup. We put it over Frank like a hood. It covered up most of his face. All you could see was a big guy with a blanket over his head.

"After we take care of you at Orly, I'm saying goodbye," he growled.

"Hey, what about all the money you can make playing basketball?" I said.

He shrugged. "What good is it if I have to go around wearing a blanket over my head?"

I looked around. There were about a million people walking around. Some were going up to see the tower. Others were coming out. "Relax," I told him. "Nobody knows you're around."

Frank nodded. "If I take this blanket off my head, they'll know it. You'll see a million people running for their lives. Or for mine."

Dr. Stein snapped his fingers. "Do not worry about it, Frank. I will make you another face."

"Thanks, doc," Frank said. "Now I have something else to worry about."

I looked around. There were signs in French, but I couldn't read them. Dr. Stein read them to us. I paid attention so that I could tell the kid sister about it.

Alexandre Gustave Eiffel built it. It took exactly two years, two months, and two days, from January 26, 1887 to March 31, 1889.

It was 1,050 feet high. It weighed 7,000 tons and had 15,000 pieces of welded metal. It was the highest building in the world until 1929, when they built the Chrysler Building in New York.

Alexandre Eiffel himself walked to the top. There were only 1,710 steps. There were three floors, the first at 187 feet, the second at 377 feet, and the third at 899 feet.

Dr. Stein took out some money. Frank and I followed him to the elevators.

The tower slanted at an angle. The lift went up really slowly. We got off at the middle platform to change cars. This one went straight up to the top.

Frank stood in the back, the blanket hooding his face. Nobody noticed him.

At the top the people scattered, running to this side and the other. Some had cameras, and they were taking shots of the view.

Dr. Stein took my arm. "Come along, Jack. From the top here, you can see forty-five miles. You will see all of Paris."

He headed for the end railing. I took one step and stopped. All of a sudden, I forgot all about seeing Paris.

Somebody was standing near the north side. I blinked in the late afternoon sun. He was wearing a lot of colors, a red hat and a blue coat. Under that was a pink dress. And there were black shoes.

There was only one more thing to check. I did that.

He had the red beard!

Alphonse! My old friend Al. There he was, not ten feet from me, on top of the Eiffel Tower in Paris!

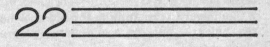

22

I walked over to Frank. I told him the story fast. He looked puzzled.

"It's got a dress and also a red beard. What is it, a man or a woman?"

"I don't know," I said. "All I know is the last time I saw him, he said his French name was Alphonse."

Frank looked around. "You said there was another guy with him in the car."

"Gaston," I said. "They were Alphonse and Gaston."

Frank grinned. "Those are old comedy names, Jack. An old French act, you know."

"I don't know about that," I said. "But maybe he's waiting for the other dude now. What do you think?"

Frank rubbed his big hands together. He

smiled. "I think your problems will be over soon, Jack."

"They have to confess first," I said. "How can I get them to tell the people at Orly how they bring in the pot?"

Frank nodded. "Just tell me when the other one gets here. Will you know him?"

I shrugged. "Maybe. If I see them together again."

The elevator door opened. More people came out. One was wearing dark glasses. He walked over to the dude in the red beard and red hat and blue coat and pink dress and black shoes.

I gave Frank a nod. "That's him."

Frank smiled. "Well, go on over. See if you can get them to put you right with the law."

I walked over to where they were standing together. "Hey," I said. "Remember me?"

The two stared. "Who are you?" Alphonse said.

"I'm the dummy who brought you your birthday cake, remember? The one that was pot instead."

He looked at Gaston who said something to him in French. "We do not know you," the man said.

"I know you," I said. "Alphonse and Gaston, right?"

They were turning away. "Beat it, kid," Alphonse said.

I tugged at his coat sleeve. "There's a friend of mine here I'd like you to meet," I said.

He looked around annoyed, and then his friend turned. They both looked surprised and then shocked out of their wits.

Frank was standing right there, without the blanket over his head!

23

They had their backs to the wall at the edge of the tower, with no place to go but down. They knew it.

"It is not possible," Alphonse said.

"*C'est impossible!*" Gaston said.

"I don't know about that," I said. "You dudes are bad dudes. You ruined my trip with the Glop Oil lady. Your friend in the states faked me out with that birthday cake. I'm willing to tell my friend here to go away, if you guys are willing to tell the customs man at Orly it was your idea. Not mine."

They kept staring up at Frank. They kept saying they didn't believe it. But they were frozen stiff. The only things that moved were their teeth. They were chattering.

"It is not possible," Alphonse said again. "He is not real, this one."

"Okay, Frank," I said. "I'll hold your blanket. Maybe you can show them you're for real."

Frank smiled. He pushed his big arms out. He picked up Alphonse in one hand. He picked up Gaston with the other. The way he did it looked so easy. I wondered what he was going to do with them next.

Maybe he can shake it out of them, I told myself.

Dr. Stein came over. He saw Frank holding up the two bad dudes. "What is going on?" he asked.

"These are the guys who got me grounded at Orly airport," I said. "They don't think Frank is for real."

Dr. Stein drew himself up proudly. He looked at them sternly. "Of course, he is real. My name is Dr. Stein. I made him myself."

Alphonse and Gaston looked at him. They looked beat.

"Show them the view of Paris, Frank," Dr. Stein said.

Frank grinned. He swung them around and leaned out over the railing. Their heads were down looking at the ground. I could see people below looking like ants.

"Try not to drop them, Frank," Dr. Stein said. "We will need a confession from them."

Alphonse and Gaston were yelling. The words got lost in the wind. Frank swung them back. He laid them down.

Dr. Stein took out a notebook and pen. "Now we will hear your confession," he said.

It was a good idea. Only it didn't work.

Alphonse and Gaston had fainted!

24

I put the blanket back to cover Frank's face. "Tough luck, Jack," he said. "I thought that would do it."

"Me, too," I said. "Maybe they'll talk when they wake up."

Frank shook his head. "Maybe. And maybe not. There's a lot of people up here. What if these two start yelling about who they think I am. There will be some kind of riot."

I looked toward the elevators. "Maybe we can bring them down. Call the police."

Frank grinned. "They won't like me, either. I have a better idea."

Dr. Stein was still looking over Alphonse and Gaston. He was waiting for them to wake up and start talking.

Frank went over. He picked them up again. One under each arm. He nodded to me. "You can help, Jack," he said. "Open that door."

I looked at the door. A sign over it said:

STAIRCASE. "That's a lot of steps, Frank," I said. "Over seventeen hundred steps."

He nodded and began walking with them. "It's okay. If my arms get tired, I'll drop them."

25

It was a good idea, better than taking the car down. Nobody else was using the steps. The sign at the bottom was for real. I counted them on the way. It came to 1,710 steps.

Frank made it look easy. I guess after you lift horses and cows for a living, carrying two dudes isn't much. When we got to the bottom, a guard looked at us.

"I am a doctor," Dr. Stein said. "These men became sick at the top."

The guard nodded. He let us pass.

Frank carried them to the pickup. It was getting dark. He put them in the back of the pickup. The big box of Dr. Stein's came in handy. Frank dumped the two dudes in. He tied the lid on loosely with ropes.

Dr. Stein got behind the wheel, smiling. He waved a map. He handed it to me. "You want to go to Orly. Tell me how to go."

I unfolded the map. It was written in French. But to the south I saw the word. I waved my arm. "Orly is that way, doc. Take a left."

26

We headed south, left of the setting sun. Soon we saw signs to Orly airport. Traffic got heavy. It got dark. I heard thunder. There were flashes of lightning. A big storm was chasing us in.

We got there before it broke. The bright beams of the searchlights made the airport easier to find. Dr. Stein wasn't the world's greatest driver. But he did the job.

He headed for the curb outside the airport building. The sign in front said: NO PARKING. "Keep going," I said. "You'll get a ticket parking here."

Dr. Stein shook his head. He parked anyway. "The sign is in English, my boy. The police will think I read only French."

We got out. Frank jumped up in the back and went to the big box. The dudes inside were making sounds. Banging on the box. They were yelling, "Let us out!"

Frank slid back the cover. He grinned down at them. They stopped yelling. Seeing that face could cool anybody. Frank pulled the box out over the open tailgate. Then he put the box on his shoulder. He began walking.

He was close to the door when I remembered his blanket. I ran to cover him. Frank shook his head.

"Forget it," he said. "Get me in the door."

I ran through first. Frank went by, carrying the big box with the two bad dudes inside. The box was wide. It hit the wall. Some of the wall came off. It didn't bother Frank.

The airport was crowded. People were looking at us. Me with my ball. Dribbling it. *Bounce bounce bounce.* Dr. Stein marching along. Swinging his cane. Frank behind us with the big box over his head. We must have looked like some kind of parade.

I saw the sign. CUSTOMS. STOP HERE FOR INSPECTION.

I pointed it out to Frank. "Straight ahead, Frank," I said.

He nodded, following me. "It will help if we find your man, Jack, the same one who found the pot you had."

I looked and didn't see him. Fuzz people were coming over. They saw Frank's face and stopped. I was getting nervous. If I didn't find the same man, there was going to be trouble.

I heard the whistle. *Beep beep.*

The man found me.

I pointed him out to Frank. "This will be fun," Frank said.

There was a long line of people at the checkpoint. They saw Frank and gave him a lot of room. The man at the counter had the whistle in his mouth. He was ready to blow me and Frank down.

Then he got his first good look at Frank. The whistle fell out of his mouth.

"Hi," I said. "How are you doing?"

Frank lifted the box high over his head. He turned it over. The two dudes fell out. The man from customs looked even more surprised.

"Okay, Frank," I said. "Maybe you ought to wait in the truck."

Frank grinned. He walked away. *Clomp clomp clomp*. He held his arms out like he was a robot, making the people think he was you-know-who. He was scaring heck out of them.

Alphonse and Gaston lay on the counter blinking. They looked scared. The customs man waited for me to tell him something.

"I told you it wasn't my idea about that birthday cake that turned out to be pot, mister," I said. "Here are the dudes who made the deal. Maybe they will tell you about it."

The man from customs smiled. He found his whistle. He waved his arms and made the *beep beep* sound. The fuzz came running.

Dr. Stein tapped his chest. "I am Dr. Stein,"

he told the man. "I will explain every-thing."

The man looked at me. "You better believe it," I said.

27

The customs man told Dr. Stein and me to wait in his office. When he came back, he was wearing a smile.

He waved a sheet of paper. "You are a big hero, my boy," he said.

"How did I become a hero?" I said.

"The two men told us everything. They are crooks. They were bringing in the dope. We hear that they picked up a man in the States. So you have broken up a very big smuggling ring, my boy."

I felt better. I started to get up.

"There is one thing more," he said.

I sat down again. It has to be that parking ticket, I thought.

He waved his arm. The door opened. A nice looking chick came in. She was smiling at me.

I turned to Dr. Stein. "It's my Glop Oil lady," I said.

He was frowning. "She is very pretty, yes. But too old for you, my boy."

The chick was getting me up on my feet. She was ready to hug me. "Glop Oil is proud of you, Jack," she said. "You are a hero. Now, if you are ready, we will begin your free trip to Paris."

The customs man waved his hand. "There is just one more thing," he said.

"The parking sign is in English," I said. "Dr. Stein only reads French."

He looked puzzled. "What does parking have to do with this? I am talking about the monster. The one who came in with you. We cannot have him going around loose, my boy. He is a menace. You must tell us where he is."

The door opened behind him. A voice came with it. "Look around," Frank said. "I'm right here."

28

I looked up at him. It was Frank, but I didn't know him.

Dr. Stein stood up. "Frank," he said. "What have you done with my face?"

Frank was rubbing it. Little bits came off. The wig was gone. So was most of the monster face.

"It was raining outside, doc. The stuff you put on my face must have melted. Hey, how do I look?"

The customs man shook his head. "I do not understand. What have you done with the other man?"

Dr. Stein thumped his chest. "I am Dr. Stein. I made the other face. This one is his own."

He helped Frank get more of the gook off. It was a lot of putty and bits of wood and cloth. Frank was beginning to look more and more like his circus poster picture.

The Glop Oil lady turned to me. "Who is your friend?"

"Oh," I said. "This is Frank Frank. He picked up the two bad dudes for me. Frank used to be the circus strongman."

"Really?" the Glop Oil lady said. "How interesting!" She opened her bag. "Your skin looks raw, Frank. Did you have an accident?"

Frank grinned. "One of the best. It made me a new man."

She was opening a small bottle. "Put some of this on your face. It's very good for the skin."

"What is it?" Frank asked.

"Glop Oil," she said. "Hold still. I'll put some on you myself." She had to reach up. "My, you're big," she said. "Were you really a circus strongman?"

"Well, I was. Now I have to find a new job." He rubbed his face. "Hey, that stuff feels good."

"How would you like a job working for us at Glop Oil, Frank?" she said.

Frank looked at me. "Well," he told her. "I was thinking about going into the NBA. Playing basketball, you know. Jack here said he could get me the job."

"How much were they going to pay you?" she said.

"Oh, about a million dollars," Frank said.

She smiled. "Well, you can get almost the same money working for us. And you won't have to do all that running up and down."

Frank said, "What do I have to do for it?"

"We'll just send you to different places, showing people how strong you are. They'll think you got that way using our Glop Oil."

Frank looked at me. "What do you think, Jack?"

"Take the money," I said.

Frank held his hand out to the lady. "I'll take it."

"Wonderful," she said. She got on her toes and kissed him. "That's good oil," she said.

Dr. Stein began to cry. "I have lost my little boy again," he said. "Goodbye, Frank. Goodbye, Jack."

"Don't feel too badly, doc," I said. "Maybe you'll find another accident case near that mountain. Next time, you can try a new kind of person."

He clapped his hands together. "The idea comes to me now. Next time, what I make will be different for sure. He will be the strongest man in the world. He will be able to fly in the air. Jump over high buildings. He will be super in every way."

"How about faster than a speeding bullet," I said.

Dr. Stein hugged me. "That, too. Thank you, my boy."

"Just don't have him wear a cape," I said.

"Why not?" Dr. Stein said. "I like the cape idea."

"Yeah," I said. "I was afraid of that."

29

It all worked right this time. The Glop Oil lady gave me the tour. I saw all of Paris. I took notes to remember everything for the kid sister.

I told the Glop Oil lady I really hadn't seen the view yet from the Eiffel Tower. "You'll love it," she said.

Frank came along. She wanted him to get used to the Glop Oil people, she said. She spent a lot of time holding his hand. Frank was getting used to it fast.

The view from the top was great. You could see for about fifty miles in any direction. Then it was time to go.

I grabbed Frank's free arm. "Hey, man," I said. "I really want to thank you for what you did here last time. Holding those two bad dudes out over the end there got me off the hook."

"It's okay," Frank said. "But I have to thank you."

"How come?" I said.

He looked down at his big hands. "Well," he said, "you know, I used to be the circus strongman. But while I was laid up with Dr. Stein I wasn't doing any lifting. So, with those two guys, it was the first chance I had. You know, to see if I got weaker, or what."

"You mean, you might have dropped them?" I said.

"Well, we had to find out, didn't we?" Frank said.

30

When I got home, the kid sister looked happy to see me. "Thanks for the postcard you sent me. That Eiffel Tower looks awfully high."

"You better believe it. It's over a thousand feet. It has seventeen hundred and ten steps."

"Terrific." She looked around. "I don't see your ball."

"Oh, that. Yeah. I gave it to Frank."

"Frank who?"

"Frank Frank. Honest, that's his name."

"Okay. So how come you gave him your ball?"

"He was getting married to the Glop Oil lady. It was a wedding present. He did me a really good favor on the trip."

"Did you have a good time?"

"It was hairy at times, but it turned out okay. I'll tell you all about it. What's been happening here? You look as if you're over the mumps."

"Yeah. Well, I've been busy. I mean, you can't just sit around doing nothing with the mumps, you know."

"I guess not," I said.

She handed me an envelope. "So here is what's been happening."

I looked at her. "Another one?"

"Congratulations, Jack. You have just won another free trip."

I opened the envelope. There it was, free tickets for winning another contest. This time it was, in fifty words or less, why she liked Doodle Mosquito Bite Lotion best.

The kid sister had done it again.

"Hey," I said. "Where is Slobovia?"

Susie shrugged. "I don't know. I was kind of hoping you would tell me."

"Hey, wait!" I said. "Isn't that where Dracula lived?"

"Well," she said, "nobody knows, for sure."

"It figures," I said.